For Zdenka Korínková

First published 1984 by
Walker Books Ltd.
17-19 Hanway House,
Hanway Place, London W1P 9DL

© 1984 Nicola Bayley

First printed 1984
Printed and bound by
L.E.G.O., Vicenza, Italy

British Library Cataloguing in Publication Data
Bayley, Nicola
Parrot cat.–(Copycats)
I. Title II. Series
823'.914[J] PZ7

ISBN 0-7445-0152-0

PARROT CAT

Nicola Bayley

If I were a parrot
instead of a cat,

I would live
in the jungle,

I would fly
through the trees,

I would be
coloured so bright,

I would sit
on my nest,

I would talk
and squawk,

and if a snake
ever came,

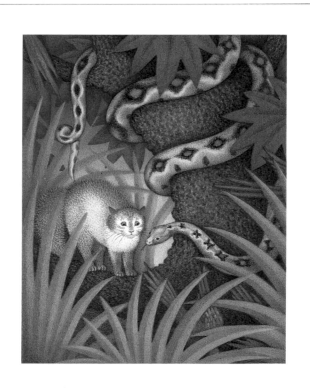

I would quickly
turn back into
a cat again.